BUZZZZZZZZZZZZZZZ
mmmm

What's That Sound, Woolly Bear?

Written by Philemon Sturges
Illustrated by Joan Paley

Little, Brown and Company

BOSTON   NEW YORK   TORONTO   LONDON

Some bugs, like Woolly Bear, wander around quietly looking for a snug place to sleep.

woolly bear

Some bugs dart.

ZIT·
ZAT
ZEEEEE

dragonfly

Some bumble.

BUZZ

BUZZZZ

bumblebee

But Woolly Bear just huffle-shuffles along
without making a sound.
Listen!
Can you hear her?

Some bugs chirp.

cricket

Some bugs skate.

DASH

DART

water bug

But Woolly Bear just huffle-shuffles through the grass. She likes to hear her friends, but what she really wants to listen to is tiger moths!

Some bugs whine.

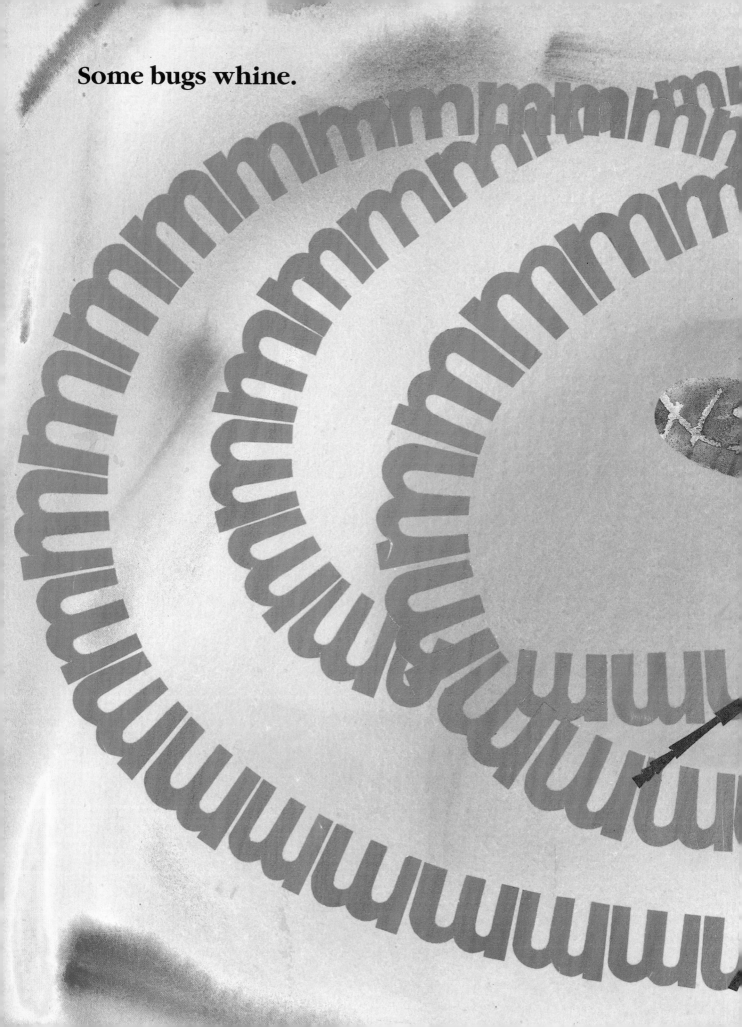

mosquito

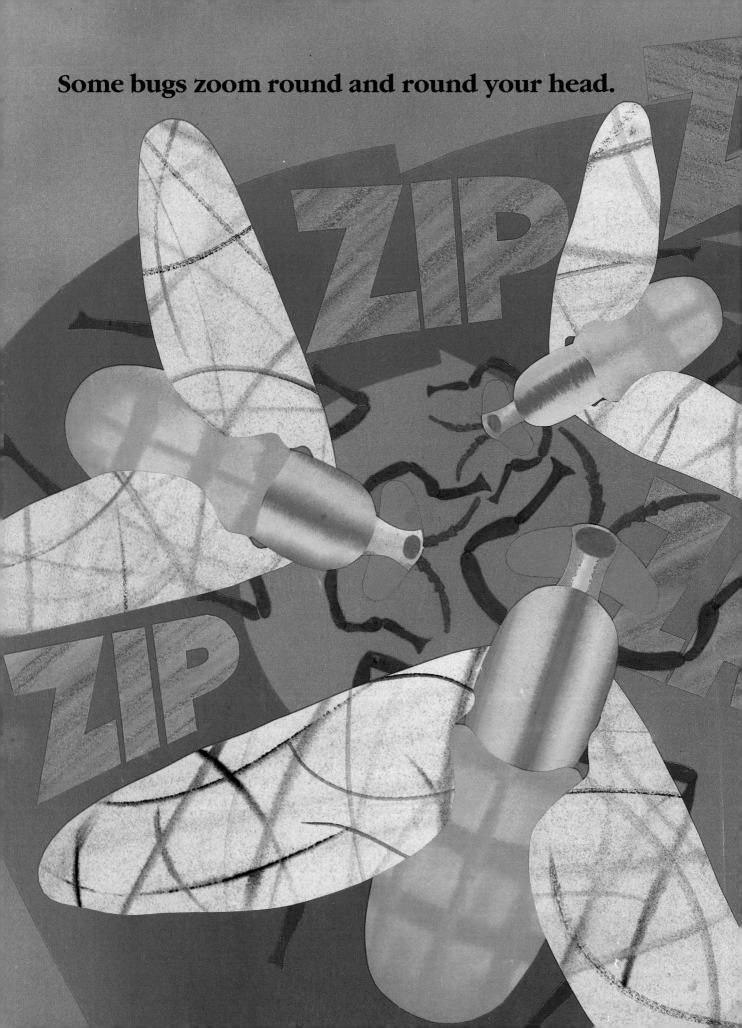

ZIP!

deerfly

Some you can hardly hear or see at all.

Ouch! They're there!

SWA

no-see-um

**But Woolly Bear just huffle-shuffles
along without bothering anybody.**

Some bugs snap away
when you get near.

ZIK

ZIK
ZIK
ZIKKERRR

Look!
There goes one!

grasshopper

Some bugs bang.

SMASH!!!...
RRRRRR
RASH!!!...
BASH!!!...

june bug

Some *whirrrr* very quietly in the night and flash.

BLINK

firefly

But Woolly Bear just huffle-shuffles into some leaves.

She's looking for a quiet place
to spin her bed and dream.

Good night, Woolly Bear.

WHIF-WHAF

Look! Beautiful Woolly Bear's turned into
a tiger moth! Can you hear her now?

Fly away, Woolly Bear!

ABOUT BUGS

There are more kinds of bugs on earth than all other types of creatures put together. Their skeletons are on the outside, so they can't grow without shedding their skin. Many bugs, such as moths, have four lives. Moths start as an egg, then hatch into a larva — called a caterpillar. The caterpillar eats until it's very fat. Then it spins a silken nest called a cocoon, becomes a pupa, and goes to sleep. When it wakes up, it's a moth! It flies away, finds its mate, lays its eggs, and dies. The eggs hatch, and it all starts over again!

WOOLLY BEARS are the caterpillars of the Isabella tiger moth. Like all creatures, they have a long Latin name: *Isia Isabella*. You usually see them in the late autumn. Their long spiky hair makes it difficult for birds to swallow them. If you catch one, it will curl up into a tight little ball and tickle your hand. Unlike most caterpillars, the woolly bear (like a real bear) sleeps all winter and wakes up in the spring. It eats a bit, then becomes a pupa, and then, in a few weeks, an Isabella.

DRAGONFLIES were here long before dinosaurs. They have four wings that move separately, so they can fly forward and backward. They do have legs, but they use them only for perching and catching bugs. They usually eat while flying! Dragonflies are good to have around because they are fond of eating flies and mosquitoes.

There are many different kinds of **WATER BUGS**. There are water striders and water scorpions, which walk delicately on the surface; and there are water beetles and water boatmen, which swim underwater or row on the surface. Some of these, such as the eastern toe-biter, bite; so be careful!

BUMBLEBEES live in colonies in the ground. There are three kinds of bees in a colony: the queen, drones, and workers. What you're most likely to see is the worker. Watch out — it stings. In the fall, the new queens and drones (the male bees) appear and mate. The drones and workers die, but the queen finds a new nest and spends the winter there. In the spring, her eggs hatch and a new colony is born.

Male **CRICKETS** love to sing. They do this by rubbing their wings together. On hot summer nights, crickets chirp in unison. You can tell how hot it is in degrees Fahrenheit by subtracting forty from the number of chirps per minute, dividing by four, and then adding fifty.

CICADAS live in trees, so you hardly ever see them. But you've probably heard the rhythmic buzzing of these "dog-day bugs" on hot summer days. There are many different kinds of cicadas. Perhaps the strangest of all bugs is the *Magicicada.* After these insects hatch, they burrow into the ground and live there for seventeen years (thirteen in the south). Then they all burst forth at once. There are so many of them that all the bug-eating creatures have a great feast but still millions are left over to sing, mate, and lay their eggs. What a symphony!

Male FIREFLIES light up the summer nights as they fly around looking for mates. The wingless females, sometimes called glow worms, sit and flash back. Every once in a while, all the fireflies in a tree or field will flash at once like a silent bolt of lightning.

Female **DEERFLIES**, like horseflies, zip around your head looking for just the right place to land and get a good meal. They are fond of large, short-haired mammals, such as deer, moose, and horses. Humans aren't as tasty, but they'll do.

JUNE BUG larvae live underground for up to three years, eating roots. The adults emerge from their pupae throughout the summer. They feed at night, are attracted to light, and are loud and clumsy fliers. They don't stop easily — they crash!

Female **MOSQUITOES** like you, even if you don't like them! The males suck plant juice and wait for the females to find a drop of blood so they can mate. On hot days, their eggs hatch in sixteen hours. The larvae live underwater. They drop to the bottom to eat and come to the surface to breathe. After seven or eight days, they become pupae, and about two days later, they become adults. Then they fly away to look for you!

NO-SEE-UMS, also called punkies or biting midges, are so small they can slip through the mesh of ordinary screens. You don't hear them until they fly into your ear — which they often do. They bite!

Short-horned **GRASSHOPPERS** are sometimes called locusts. When they fly, they flash brightly colored underwings and make a startling snapping sound. The female deposits eggs in pods in the ground, where they stay for the winter. In the spring, the young grasshoppers hatch. Sometimes they fly by the millions in swarms, and when they land, they eat everything that grows.

Note: All bugs are pictured to scale except the tiger moth and no-see-um.

To Uncle Monty, who opened the door to Mother Earth's treasure trove for me
— P. S.

To Judy-Sue, who gives, is true and faithful

For Norman, Jennifer, Jeff, and Nicholas, my loves
— J. P.

Text copyright © 1996 by Philemon F. Sturges
Illustrations copyright © 1996 by Joan Paley

First Edition

Library of Congress Cataloging-in-Publication Data

Sturges, Philemon.
    What's that sound, Woolly Bear? / written by Philemon Sturges ;
illustrated by Joan Paley. — 1st ed.
    p.   cm.
    Summary: Woolly Bear quietly shuffles along, looking for a place to
spin her bed and dream of tiger moths, while all around her other
bugs buzz, chatter, zip, and whir.
    ISBN 0-316-82021-0
    [1. Caterpillars — Fiction. 2. Insects — Fiction. 3. Animal
sounds — Fiction.]   I. Paley, Joan, ill.   II. Title.
PZ7.S9414Wh 1996
[E] — dc20   95-5427

                10 9 8 7 6 5 4 3 2 1

                            NIL

Published simultaneously in Canada
by Little, Brown & Company (Canada) Limited

*The collages in this book are a combination of cut paper, watercolor,
crayon, and pastel. Watercolor washes along with crayon and pastel
line were applied to textured and/or colored papers, which were then
cut and layered to create a three-dimensional effect.*

Printed in Italy